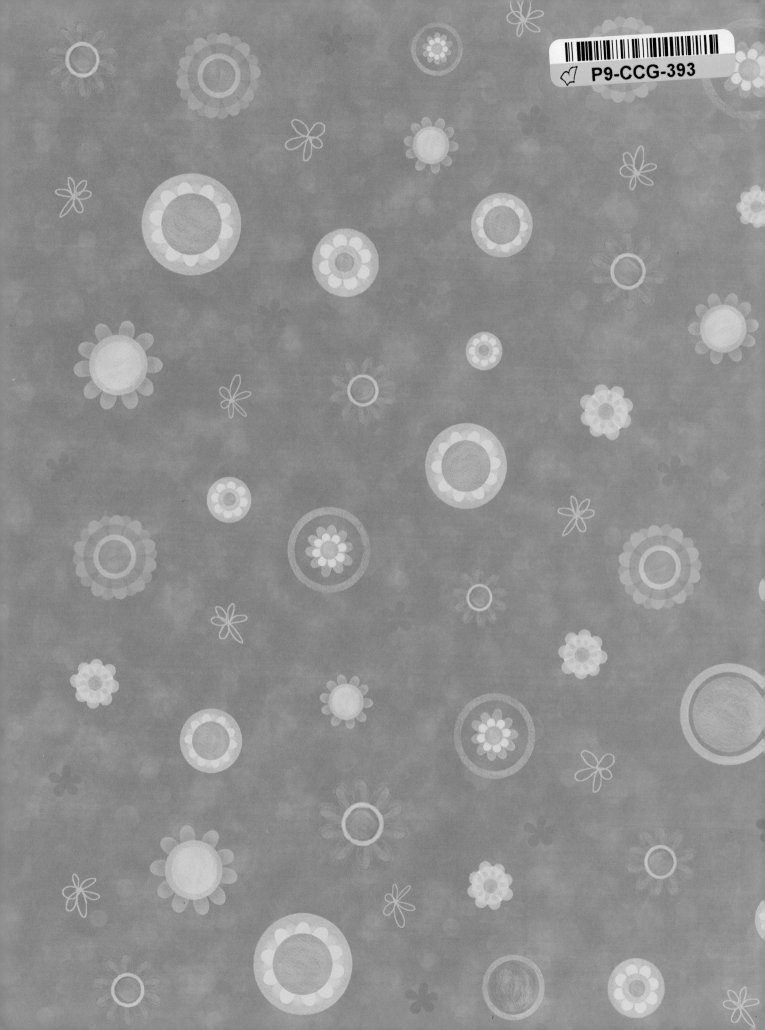

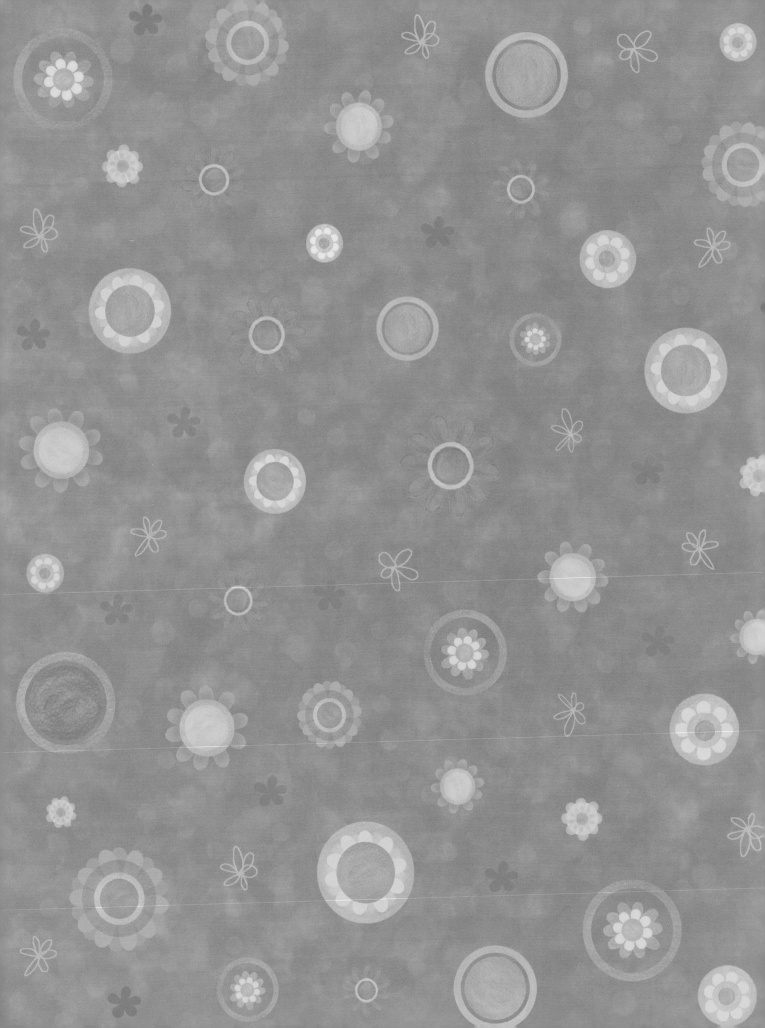

Hello, Sun!

Sounds True
Boulder, CO 80306

Illustrations and text © 2019 by Sarah Jane Hinder

Published 2019

Cover & jacket design by Jennifer Miles
Illustrations by Sarah Jane Hinder

Printed in South Korea

Library of Congress Cataloging-in-Publication Data
Names: Hinder, Sarah Jane, author, illustrator.
Title: Hello, sun! : a yoga sun salutation to start your day / written and
   illustrated by Sarah Jane Hinder.
Description: Boulder, CO : Sounds True, 2019. | Summary: Illustrations and
   simple, rhyming text introduce a sun salutation yoga sequence for
   children.
Identifiers: LCCN 2018050875 (print) | LCCN 2018055062 (ebook) | ISBN
   9781683642848 (ebook) | ISBN 9781683642831 (hardcover)
Subjects: | CYAC: Stories in rhyme. | Yoga--Fiction.
Classification: LCC PZ8.3.H5553 (ebook) | LCC PZ8.3.H5553 Hel 2019
(print) |
   DDC [E]--dc23
LC record available at https://lccn.loc.gov/2018050875

10 9 8 7 6 5 4 3 2 1

Hello, Sun!

A Yoga Sun Salutation
to Start Your Day

Sarah Jane Hinder

sounds true
BOULDER, COLORADO

Stand tall as a mountain.

Reach high as can be.

Bow down to the ground.
What do you see?

Step back and gaze forward,
saluting the sky.

Warm light shining brightly
and clouds floating by.

Be a strong bridge,
focused and steady.

Lower knees, chest, and chin
as soon as you're ready.

Push up to the sun,
shining warmth on your face.

Exhale, touch your toes,
smile, and stretch into place.

Step into the light
and open your heart.

Swan dive to the earth,
feet slightly apart.

Raise your arms into prayer
as you greet the new day.

Return back to Mountain.

Kind
thoughts

Kind
words

Kind
heart

Exhale. Namaste.

The sunlight in me sees the sunlight in you!

Hello, Sun!
FLOW

Extended Mountain Pose
Breathe in

From Mountain Pose, raise your arms up towards the sky, lifting your chin at the same time. If you are feeling flexible, you might want to lean further back for a gentle backbend.

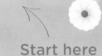

Mountain Pose
Breathe in and out three times to begin

Stand with your feet together, arms by your sides. With your big toes touching and heels slightly apart, lift your toes up towards the sky and feel an equal balance under your feet. Roll your shoulders back and pull in your belly. Stand still and tall. Breathe in and out slowly.

Mountain Pose
Breathe in and out three times to end

Start here

The flow on this page is a half round of a sun salutation. Complete this flow, leading with your right leg. Then do the flow again, leading with your left leg. Three full rounds are a good number to practice, but you can do as many or as few as you want. You can be as slow or as fast as you want. Remember to focus on your breathing and have fun!

How many rounds can you do?

Extended Mountain Pose
Breathe in

Standing Forward Fold
Breathe out

Low Lunge
Breathe in

Standing Forward Fold
Breathe out

From Extended Mountain Pose, reach high up to the sky and then fold forward, taking your hands to the floor at the sides of your feet. If you need to, bend your knees so your hands can touch the floor.

Low Lunge
Breathe in

From Standing Forward Fold, step forward with your right foot and lower your back knee to the ground. Remember to keep your upper body tall.

Plank
Hold breath

From Low Lunge, step both feet back and hold your body strong and straight. Keep your thighs and bottom tight and your neck tall and long in line with your spine.

Eight Point Pose
Breathe out

From Plank Pose, drop your knees to the ground and lift your bottom up to the sky to create a slight bend in your back. Slowly lower your body towards the ground, keeping your elbows tucked into your sides. You are aiming to touch the ground with your chin and chest.

Cobra
Breathe in

From Eight Point Pose, push your upper body up with your hands, keeping elbows tucked into your sides. Keep your neck long and tall, with your shoulders back, and gaze forward. Feet should be slightly apart.

Downward-Facing Dog
Breathe out

From Cobra, keep your hands facing forward, shoulder width apart. Lift your bottom up to the sky as you place your feet on the ground, hip width apart. Press your heels towards the ground. Keep your arms strong and straight with your neck long and tall in line with your spine.

Step forward with right leg first.

Repeat flow, stepping forward with left leg.

What Are Sun Salutations?

A long time ago, in India, a group of people practiced yoga. They were called yogis. They worshipped and celebrated the sun, as they knew how important it was. The sun gives us light, warmth, and energy. The yogis used to do 108 Sun Salutations before the rest of their yoga practice to warm up their bodies and calm their minds.

Sun Salutations, also known as Surya Namaskar, are a sequence of twelve yoga poses that we follow to warm up our bodies. Sun Salutations are often practiced in the morning to give us lots of energy for the rest of the day.

Today we know that the sun is the life source for this planet. Its energy is in everything that we eat, drink, and breathe. Sunshine makes us feel happy. Practicing Sun Salutations makes our bodies and minds happy and healthy too.

Sunshine Meditation

Lie down on your back and make yourself
comfortable and still. Close your eyes,
take a big breath in, and slowly breathe out.

Let your body feel soft and relaxed. Imagine
you are floating on a big, fluffy cloud. You can
hear the birds tweeting, the hum of buzzing bees,
and the flutter of butterfly wings. Imagine the warmth
of the sun on your face.

With your eyes closed, slowly start to rub your hands together and feel them
getting warmer. Imagine the energy from the golden sun. Place your hands on
your tummy. What do you feel? Move your hands to your chest and fill your
heart with the sun's warm, yellow light. Can you feel your heart beating? Feel the
warmth spread like an orange glow across your arms and down your legs. Breathe
in the light and think, "I am love." Feel the sunshine's rays warming your body.
You are shining bright. Breathe in the sunlight and think, "I am sunshine."

Let's wake up your body by wiggling your fingers and toes. Lift your arms up to
the sky and then reach them back behind your head. Point your fingers and toes
and have a big stretch and a yawn. Bring your knees up to your chest and give
yourself a big hug, rocking side to side. Slowly roll onto your right side and then
quietly come to a seated position. Open your eyes and feel ready for the new day.
Breathe in and think, "I am happy."

To Mila and Finn,
my little rays of sunshine

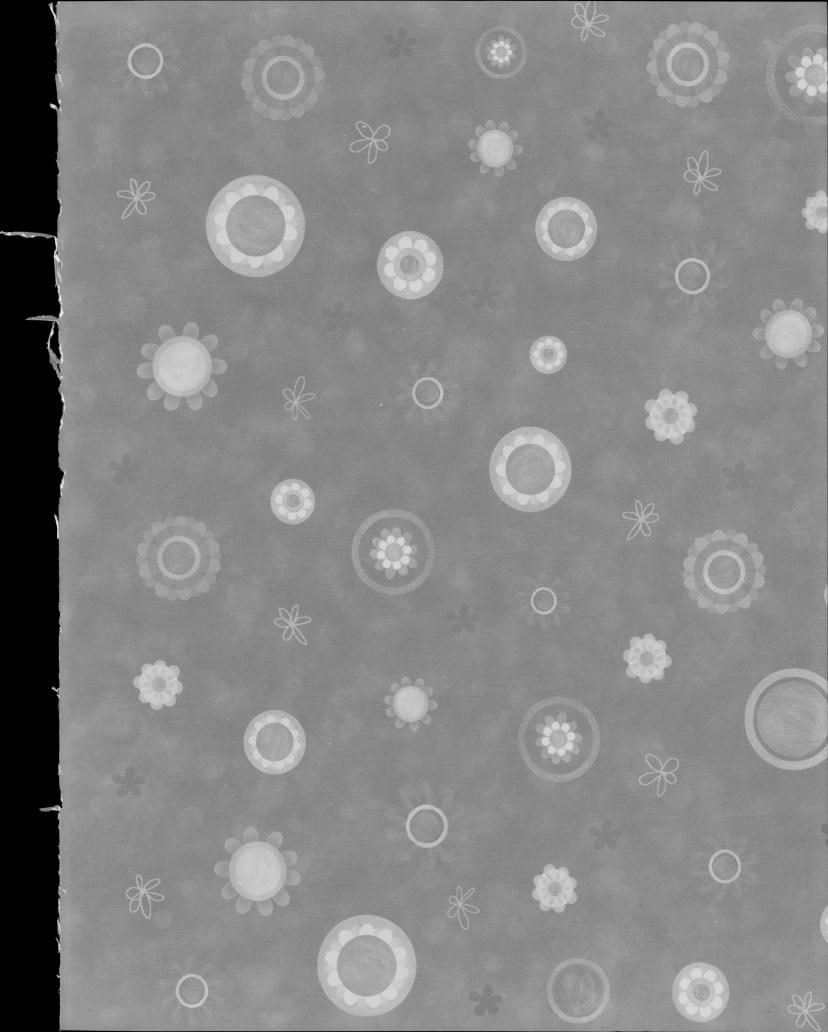

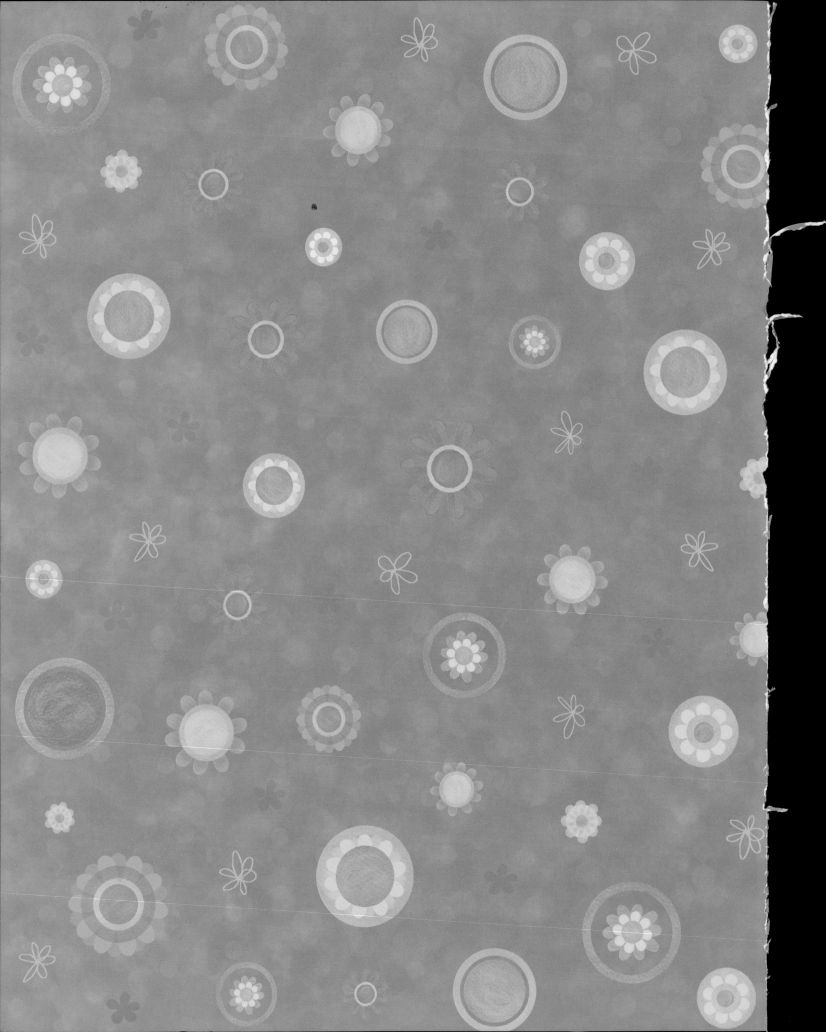